What Can
I Write?

A Red Fox Book

Published by Random House Children's Books
20 Vauxhall Bridge Road, London SW1V 2SA

A division of Random House UK Ltd
London Melbourne Sydney Auckland
Johannesburg and agencies throughout the world

Copyright © Martina Selway 1997

1 3 5 7 9 10 8 6 4 2

First published in Great Britain by
Hutchinson Children's Books 1997

Red Fox edition 1998

Printed in Singapore

RANDOM HOUSE UK Limited Reg. No. 954009

ISBN 0 09 921372 9

What Can I Write?

Martina Selway

Red Fox

London Sydney Auckland Johannesburg

For Jane Hamilton-Selway

With thanks to Sarah White and to the pupils of Chandlers Field School, West Molesey, Surrey, for their drawings.

Rosie's teacher has asked the class to write
a story about what they did in the holidays.
Rosie can't think of a single thing. She hadn't
been anywhere. She hadn't done anything.
  She asked, "What can I write?"
  Miss West said, "Come on, Rosie, just start!"

The first day of my holiday Mum was working.
I had to go to Mrs. Benn's, next door. I don't
like Mrs. Benn much and I didn't like what
she cooked for lunch. It was horrible liver
and onions and cabbage. I wouldn't eat it.
Mrs. Benn said, "Children today don't know
what's good for them."
She gave it to her cat Lilly and I had a
cheese sandwich. Afterwards I played with
Lilly while Mrs. Benn was knitting. Lilly got
the wool in a terrible mess!
When Mum came back to get me
she promised we'd go to the
Toy Museum next day.

Next morning when I opened the curtains it was raining really hard. The sky was very dark and there was thunder and lightning. I waited for it to stop all morning.

Mum said, "It's no good, Rosie. We can't go out today. It's raining cats and dogs!"

I was <u>so</u> bored that Mum let me watch television all afternoon. Then in the middle of my favourite programme, smoke came out of the back of the TV! It made a crackly noise and went blank. We rang the repairers but they couldn't come. We rang my friend Roland Roberts, but he wasn't there. I wanted to make biscuits, but we hadn't got any flour.

I thought we would go to the Toy Museum today,
but we had to wait for the TV to be repaired.
Roland came round. I got out all my toys
to play a proper game but Roland only
wanted to play with his new Game boy.
He wouldn't let me have a go. We had a fight
and I got into trouble for knocking the
flowers over.
I said, "It was your fault, Roland. I hate you."
Mum yelled at us to stop squabbling. She told
us to play nicely while she made our tea.
Roland didn't stay for tea. He wanted to go
home. I was glad. At bedtime Mum said
she'd be working tomorrow and I would
have to go to Roland's!

I did not want to go to Roland's. Then Mrs. Roberts phoned and told me to bring my roller boots and we'd go to the park. It took a long time to find them as I hadn't been skating for ages. At the park Roland and I put on our boots, but mine were too small. They pinched my toes. I couldn't wear them.

Mrs. Roberts said, "Never mind, Rosie. While Roland's skating, you can feed the ducks."
She bought us scrummy ice creams.
It was fun feeding the birds, even though a greedy goose nearly ate my ice cream!
But I really wanted to be roller-skating.

I jumped on Mum's bed in the morning and shouted, "Toy Museum!" Mum said she was really sorry, but she had to visit Mrs. Jones and do her shopping. I cried. Mum told me we'd buy some flour while we were out, so that we could make some biscuits.

Mrs. Jones and her dog are very, very old. Her dog is called Skipper. He only has one eye and he doesn't play. He makes the house smell. Mrs. Jones said, "When I was your age I used to help my mother make biscuits." She gave me an old box. Inside were lots of tin shapes to cut out the biscuits. When we got home it was too late to make them.

I couldn't wait to make the biscuits next day. Mum and I weighed the flour and sugar and butter, then mixed them all together. I used Mrs. Jones's little shape cutters and put currants in some of the biscuits. Mum put them in the oven to cook. We made lots. They looked great. Then the phone rang and it was Grandad. We all had a long chat. Grandad said, "When are you coming to visit us, Old Ginger Nut? The animals are missing you."

I wished I was at Grandad's farm now. When we went back into the kitchen it was full of smoke. We'd forgotten the biscuits! They were burned black and we couldn't eat them.

Mum's friend Paula and her baby George came round at lunch time. George is really nice. I call him Chubbychops. I told Paula it was a pity we didn't have any biscuits for George. Paula said, "Don't worry, Rosie. You can give him his cauliflower cheese for lunch." Just as I gave him a ginormous spoonful, he sneezed! It went all over me.
Mum and Paula laughed, then George laughed.
I didn't think it was funny.

On Saturday we went to a big store to look for a new dress for Mum. She was going to a special party. There were rows and rows of dresses. I looked at all of them. Then when I looked for Mum I couldn't find her. It was scary. I almost cried. A girl from the shop asked if I was lost. I told her my name and she went and spoke into a microphone. You could hear her all over the place.

She said, "Will Mrs. Lee please come to the Manager's office where your daughter Rosie is waiting?"

I was so pleased to see Mum, but she looked cross and told me never to wander off like that again!

Mum looked lovely in her new dress. Sharon and her boyfriend were baby-sitting. I was looking forward to it because they're good fun. But they were in a bad mood and wouldn't play with me. While I was getting my nightie on, I heard them having a row.

Sharon shouted, "That's it, Gary. I never want to see you again."

Then Gary left and Sharon was really upset. I went and sat with her and we watched a film on TV. It was a soppy old love story and Sharon cried so much she used a whole box of Mum's tissues.

When I woke up next morning I felt shivery
and my throat hurt. Mum came in and
swished my curtains open. The light was
very bright.
Mum said, "Wake up, sleepyhead. Time to
get up. We're off to the Toy Museum today."
My nose was running and when I started
to speak my voice was all croaky. I had
a cold! Mum said it was such a shame
and gave me some horrible medicine.
She told me to stay in bed and with a bit of
luck I'd be well enough for the start of
school on Monday.
And I was!

So you see, I didn't do anything and I didn't go anywhere. I never got to make any more biscuits, I never went roller-skating and I never went to the Toy Museum.

The end.

Well done, Rosie! You found lots to write about! Guess what? Next week the class is visiting the Toy Museum!